W9-AZE-416

THE LEGEND OF
BRIGHTBLADE

ALSO BY ETHAN M. ALDRIDGE

Estranged

Estranged: The Changeling King

THE LEGEND OF
BRIGHTBLADE
ETHAN M. ALDRIDGE
Quill Tree Books
Imprints of HarperCollinsPublishers
HARPER
alley

Quill Tree Books is an imprint of HarperCollins Publishers.
HarperAlley is an imprint of HarperCollins Publishers.

The Legend of Brightblade

For information address HarperCollins Children's Books, a division of HarperCollins Publishers, 195 Broadway, New York, NY 10007.
www.harpercollinschildrens.com

ISBN 978-0-06-299552-0 (paperback)
ISBN 978-0-06-299553-7 (hardcover)

The artist used watercolors, ink, and Adobe Photoshop to create the illustrations for this book.
Typography by Ethan M. Aldridge and Molly Fehr

21 22 23 24 25 RTLO 10 9 8 7 6 5 4 3 2 1
First Edition

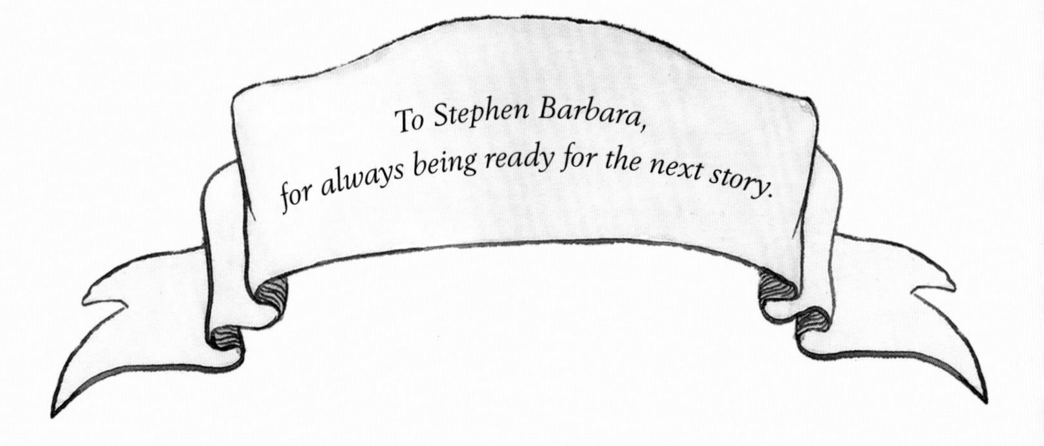
To Stephen Barbara,
for always being ready for the next story.

SK
CLIFFSID
THE RAMBLE
TROLL COUNTRY
THE TEETH
HEARTWOOD
HINDSIGHT
CORRIN
ASHEN

ALD
DAWN'S BAY
THE WATCH
THISTLEFALL
THE STARFALL SEA
AK

PROLOGUE
ASHEN PEAK

YOU ANTS... YOU'LL PAY FOR THIS.
YOU'LL *ALL* PAY!
THIS HAS TO END, *NOW*! ELUVIAN, WE NEED A DISTRACTION!
I'LL MANAGE SOMETHING.

GET READY . . .
NOW!
RRRRR!

LET'S FINISH THIS!

AAAH!

LET ME SEE, TORIL. IT'S ALL RIGHT...
CALDER...IS IT REALLY OVER? IS IT *DONE*?
YOU'LL BE ALL RIGHT, TORIL. WE ALL WILL.
HMPH. I'D SAY IT'S ABOUT AS "DONE" AS IT GETS.
SO WHAT HAPPENS NOW?
NOW? NOW I HAVE A *WHOPPER* OF A BALLAD TO WRITE!
"THE EPIC OF TORIL BRIGHTBLADE"! ALL OF SKALD IS GOING TO WANT TO HEAR IT.
NOW WE START OVER. WE PICK UP THOSE THAT NEED PICKING UP.

WE PUT THE KINGDOM BACK TOGETHER.
YOU KNOW SOMETHING? I'D LIKE TO START A FAMILY TOO.
A FAMILY?
I WANT TO MAKE IT A BETTER WORLD FOR THEM. A BETTER WORLD FOR ALL OF US.

CHAPTER 1
DAWN'S
BAY

WHERE'S YOUR BROTHER?
ALTO SNUCK OFF AFTER BREAKFAST. HE HAD HIS INSTRUMENT WITH HIM AGAIN.
HMM. I'LL HAVE A TALK WITH HIM LATER.
I GUESS THAT MEANS LESSONS ARE CANCELED FOR THE DAY?
NO, AMARA, THEY ARE NOT. IT'S IMPORTANT THAT YOU'RE ALL PREPARED TO LEAD THIS KINGDOM, AND I'M GOING TO MAKE SURE THAT HAPPENS.

NOW PUT THAT BOOK AWAY, YOUNG LADY. YOU AND ASTRID START WITH FIRST POSITION.

THE ROAD WINDS EVER FAR FOR THEE
OVER LAND AND UNDER SEA.
SO YOU'LL WANDER, EVER ONWARD,
TILL THE ROAD WINDS BACK TO ME.

WILL YOU BRING YOUR SHINING STAR HOME—
AND SHARE ITS SOFT LIGHT WITH ME? OR WALKING ONWARD, WILL YOU ROAM—
OUT THERE ACROSS THE FAR SEA.
MASTER ELUVIAN! I WAS JUST PRACTICING THE NEW PATTERNS YOU SHOWED ME.
NOT BAD, BUT YOU STILL NEED WORK ON YOUR FORCE OF WILL. THE MAGIC COULD BE SHARPER.

I SEE THAT. COME DOWN HERE AND WE'LL SEE IF WE CAN GIVE IT A LITTLE BOOST.
WATCH CLOSELY NOW—
REMEMBER SITTING IN THE GRASS, ME BESIDE THEE, NEVER FAR.
ON THAT WARM NIGHT, THE DARK BLEW PAST—
THAT WAS WHEN WE SAW THE STAR.

ITS COLOR BLAZED A GOLDEN LIGHT; THE STAR FELL PAST THE FAR SEA.
IT STOLE YOUR HEART THAT SWEET, WARM NIGHT, AND THAT WAS WHEN I LOST THEE.
WHOA...
TRUE MAGIC NEEDS FORCE OF *FEELING* AND FORCE OF *WILL* TO COME OUT RIGHT.
ANYONE WITH DETERMINATION AND A REASONABLE AMOUNT OF HEARTACHE CAN MUSTER UP THE *FEELING*.
IT TAKES A TRUE BARD TO SHAPE THE MAGIC WITH THEIR *WILL*. OTHERWISE YOU'RE JUST SHOOTING PRETTY SPARKS.
BUT I'VE BEEN WORKING ON MY WILL. I CAN'T GET IT TO COME OUT HOW YOURS DOES.
IT'S BEEN A LONG TIME SINCE I'VE TAUGHT AN APPRENTICE, ALTO, BUT I'LL TELL YOU WHAT I TOLD THEM—

IN TIME, YOUR MAGIC WILL COME IN A WAY THAT IS UNIQUE TO YOU, AND YOU'LL FIND THE FEELING AND WILL TO DO IT BY *DOING* IT, OUT THERE IN THE WORLD.
DO YOU UNDERSTAND?
YEAH, I THINK SO. BUT...COULD YOU SHOW ME THAT AGAIN, JUST TO BE SURE?
DON'T YOU HAVE OTHER LESSONS YOU SHOULD BE AT?
...NO?
ALTO.
YOU'RE BUSTED.
ASTRID IS LOOKING EVERYWHERE FOR YOU.
NOT NOW, AMARA.
TELL ASTRID I'LL CATCH UP ON LESSONS *LATER*.
LESSONS ARE OVER. WE NEED TO GET READY FOR THE DINNER TONIGHT.

DINNER?
WITH THE TROLLS. MOTHER SAID WE *ALL* HAVE TO BE THERE, REMEMBER?
UGH, ONE OF *THOSE* DINNERS.
COME ON, YOU KNOW HOW ASTRID GETS BEFORE THESE THINGS.
YOU'D BEST GET GOING.
OKAY. BUT RIGHT AFTER DINNER, I'M GOING TO MASTER THAT SPELL. JUST WATCH, YOU'LL SEE!
I'LL LOOK FORWARD TO IT.

Tch! Tch! Tch!
FOUND HIM.
THERE YOU ARE!

CHANGE OUT OF THAT RAGAMUFFIN COSTUME, *QUICK.*
I ALREADY HAVE YOUR OUTFIT PICKED OUT.
IT'S NOT A COSTUME, *ASTRID.* I'M A *BARD,* THIS IS THE KIND OF THING BARDS WEAR.
YOU ARE A *PRINCE,* AND *THIS* IS THE KIND OF THING A PRINCE WEARS.
COME ON, ALTO. THIS IS IMPORTANT. IF THIS NEGOTIATION GOES WELL, IT WILL DO *A LOT* OF GOOD FOR THE PEOPLE OF SKALD.
NOW GET DRESSED, AND WHEN YOU'RE DONE I'LL HELP YOU WITH YOUR HAIR.
MY HAIR IS *FINE,* AND I'M *NOT* PUTTING THAT ON.

WITH THE TROLLS' HELP, WE COULD PROVIDE *MUCH*-NEEDED RESOURCES FOR *HUNDREDS* OF PEOPLE.
WE'VE WORKED *HARD* OVER THE YEARS, AND SKALD IS A BETTER PLACE FOR IT...
...BUT THERE IS STILL SO MUCH THAT WE NEED TO DO.
I UNDERSTAND, BRIGHTBLADE, BUT I DON'T THINK *YOU* DO.

YOUR VILLAGERS DON'T *TRUST* US. EVEN IF WE *WANTED* THE ALLIANCE, *THEY* WOULDN'T WELCOME IT.
WE *ALL* DID THINGS DURING THE DARK YEARS WE AREN'T PROUD OF, MYSELF INCLUDED.
IT WAS A TERRIBLE TIME FOR *EVERYONE.* BUT NOW IS A TIME OF PROGRESS AND PROSPERITY!
WE HAVE AN OBLIGATION TO THE PEOPLE WITHIN OUR CHARGE TO *SPREAD* THAT PROGRESS.
AHEM.

IF WE CAN SIMPLY TEACH OUR PEOPLE TO TRUST EACH OTHER...
...WE CAN FORGE A FUTURE BRIGHTER THAN ANYTHING THIS KINGDOM HAS EVER SEEN.
HMMMMM...

ALTO...
CRAAAAACK!

OOPS.

I CAN'T OVERSTATE HOW *INCREDIBLY* LUCKY YOU ARE.
YOU'RE FORTUNATE THAT CHIEF DAGDA HAS A *HEALTHY* SENSE OF HUMOR.
IF YOU HAD PULLED YOUR LITTLE STUNT WITH ANY OTHER TROLL CLAN, THEY WOULD HAVE HAD *YOU* FOR DESSERT.
I'M SORRY, MOTHER. IT WAS AN ACCIDENT.
IT WAS *NOT*. ALTO, THIS IS *SERIOUS*.

WHAT I WAS DISCUSSING WITH CHIEF DAGDA IS IMPORTANT, NOT JUST TO ME, BUT TO HUNDREDS OF PEOPLE WHO REALLY NEED HELP.
YOU HAVE PUT ALL OF THAT AT RISK. DO YOU UNDERSTAND?
EVERYONE JUST LOOKED SO BORED, AND I WAS BORED, AND—
AND WHAT? YOU THOUGHT YOU'D PUT ON A *SHOW*?
PRACTICE MAGIC DURING DELICATE NEGOTIATIONS?
YOU ARE MY SON, AND WHEN PEOPLE SEE YOU, IT IS A REFLECTION OF ME, WHETHER YOU LIKE IT OR NOT.
YOU HAVE *RESPONSIBILITIES*, ALTO, AND I EXPECT YOU TO UPHOLD THEM.
BUT *WHY*? I WANT TO BE A *BARD*, LIKE MASTER ELUVIAN! I'VE LEARNED *SO MUCH* ABOUT MAGIC. HERE, WATCH THIS—
MASTER ELUVIAN HAS BEEN VERY GENEROUS IN INDULGING YOU, ALTO.
I'D HOPED THAT HAVING A CONSTRUCTIVE HOBBY WOULD HELP YOU BE MORE *ATTENTIVE* IN YOUR DUTIES. I SEE NOW THAT IT HAS HAD THE *OPPOSITE* EFFECT. THAT IS MY MISTAKE.

WHAT ARE YOU *SAYING?*
WE ALL HAVE RESPONSIBILITIES, ALTO. I DO, YOU DO, EVEN ELUVIAN DOES. THERE ARE OTHER THINGS I NEED HER HELP WITH NOW. I'VE ALREADY SPOKEN TO HER, AND SHE'S LEAVING *TONIGHT* ON AN IMPORTANT MISSION.
THERE ARE THINGS I NEED *YOUR* HELP WITH HERE IN THE PALACE. IT'S TIME YOUR MAGIC LESSONS END.
NO! YOU *CAN'T*!
I THINK I'VE BEEN MORE THAN UNDERSTANDING. YOU NEED TO *FOCUS*, SWEETHEART.
BUT I *AM*! ON *BEING A BARD*!
I KNOW IT'S HARD, SWEETHEART. BUT WE HAVE TO DO WHAT'S BEST FOR *EVERYONE*.

WE'RE TOO *OLD* FOR THIS.
I HATE TO SEND YOU OFF, EL, BUT I'M AFRAID OF WHAT WILL HAPPEN IF WE DON'T STRENGTHEN OUR STANDING WITH THE OTHER KINGDOMS.

WE'VE COME SO FAR, BUT IT STILL FEELS LIKE EVERYONE IS WATCHING SKALD, LOOKING FOR CRACKS.
BUT I SHOULDN'T ASK YOU TO GO ON THESE LONG JOURNEYS. MAYBE I SHOULD JUST SEND THE BRIGADE.
DON'T BE RIDICULOUS. THOSE BOYS ARE SWEET, BUT THEY HAVE NO TACT.
IF WE'RE GOING TO REBUILD RELATIONS WITH CORRIN, WHAT'S NEEDED IS WIT, CHARM, AND BEAUTY. I'M THE ONLY WOMAN FOR THE JOB.
THANKS, EL.
YOU SPOKE WITH ALTO?
HE WAS UPSET, BUT HE'LL MANAGE.
I DON'T KNOW HOW TO REACH THAT BOY SOMETIMES.

YOU KNOW, TORIL, HE REMINDS ME OF *US*...
...BEFORE ALL OF *THIS*.
WE FOUGHT *HARD* FOR ALL OF THIS, EL.
IF WE AREN'T PREPARED TO *KEEP* FIGHTING...
...IT COULD ALL SLIP AWAY IN AN INSTANT.

ALTO NEEDS TO LEARN HIS PLACE IN THAT FIGHT.
DON'T WORRY, TORIL. HE'S A CLEVER BOY.
I HAVE A FEELING HE'LL FIGURE IT OUT.

CHAPTER 2

HEY!
HEY, YOU DOWN THERE!
ARE YOU ALL RIGHT?
YEAH, THANKS, I'M FINE. WE BARDS ARE USED TO SLEEPING UNDER THE STARS.
KRICK!
A BARD, HUH? THAT'S FANCY.

ARE YOU LOST, MASTER BARD? OR ARE YOU HEADED TO THE MARKET?
YEP. YES. THE MARKET. THAT'S *DEFINITELY* WHERE I MEANT TO GO.
GOOD! I'VE GOT TO GET SET UP. PERHAPS I'LL SEE YOU THERE.
RIGHT. THANKS!

PLINK!

THE CURRENTS OF THE SEA FLOWED OUT BEFORE OUR LADY'S SHIP. SHE AMONG HER PEOPLE DEAR, HER BRIGHT BLADE AT HER HIP.
SHE WATCHED THE SHORE FOR SIGNS OF HIM, WATCHING AS THE LIGHT GREW DIM, WATCHING FOR THE AWFUL DRAGON, BONE-WHITE FROM TAIL TO TIP.
SHE DID NOT SEE THE SERPENT COME, SHE TRIED TO WATCH AND WAIT. A LOOKOUT SAW HIS DREADFUL SHAPE, HIS CRY CAME FAR TOO LATE.

THE DRAGON SHOT OUT OF THE DARK; FLYING FAST, HE HIT HIS MARK. THE SMALL FLEET TORN ASUNDER, THERE THE PEOPLE MET THEIR FATE.
HE DID NOT LET ONE SOUL ESCAPE; HE SLAUGHTERED THEM LIKE SHEEP. THE DRAGON, HAVING HAD HIS FILL, FLEW TO HIS MOUNTAIN KEEP.
HE DIDN'T SEE UPON THE TIDE HER SMALL SHAPE, HER SWORD BESIDE HER. WASHED ASHORE UPON THE SANDS, SAFE FROM THE DARK, COLD DEEP.
OUR LADY WOKE AMONG THE WRECK; HER HAIR SHONE WITH THE DAY. SHE SAT THERE AS THE TIDE CAME IN AND WASHED HER LIFE AWAY.
TILL TURNING, CLUTCHING HER BRIGHT SWORD, SHE SET OFF WEST, TRAVELING TOWARD THE MOUNTAINS. LADY BRIGHTBLADE SWORE SHE'D MAKE THE DRAGON PAY.

HEH...
CLAP!
CLAP!
CLAP!
CLAP!
VERY IMPRESSIVE, LITTLE GUY!
I LOVE THE BRIGHTBLADE BALLADS, AND I HAVEN'T SEEN MAGIC LIKE THAT IN A WHILE.
MY MAGIC HAS NEVER FELT THAT STRONG!
I DIDN'T KNOW IF IT WOULD WORK. I'VE NEVER ACTUALLY PLAYED WITH ANOTHER BARD BEFORE.
ME NEITHER. NOT A LOT OF TROLL BARDS, YOU KNOW?
WHO WAS YOUR MAGIC TEACHER?
MY, AH, MY TEACHER?
YEAH, YOU MUST HAVE TRAINED UNDER ONE OF ELUVIAN'S OLD APPRENTICES, RIGHT?

THAT MUST HAVE COST A PRETTY PENNY. I'VE HEARD THEY ONLY TAKE ON STUDENTS EVERY ONCE IN A WHILE.
RIGHT. WELL, WHO WAS *YOUR* TEACHER?
I CAN'T AFFORD THAT STUFF. I'M SELF-TAUGHT.
IT'S ALL JUST A BUNCH OF HEDGE MAGIC, BUT I'VE GOT A LOT OF FEELING TO BACK IT UP.
YOU LEARNED ALL THAT *YOURSELF*?
I JUST FEEL IT OUT, YOU KNOW? WHAT ABOUT YOU?
YEAH, I'M SELF-TAUGHT TOO. I—I FOUND A BOOK ON MAGIC A WHILE BACK AND WORKED UP FROM THERE.
REALLY? MAN, THAT IS *IMPRESSIVE*.
YOU'LL HAVE TO COME BY THE HEARTH LATER. I'D BE HAPPY TO SWAP SOME STEW FOR A FEW POINTERS.

THE HEARTH?
THE BEST HOME A GIRL COULD ASK FOR.
IT'S PARKED AT THE EDGE OF TOWN. IT'S A BRIGHT YELLOW WAGON. YOU CAN'T MISS IT.
HERE'S YOUR HALF OF THE TAKE. COME BY LATER?
YEAH, I'LL BE THERE.
GREAT! I'M EBBE, BY THE WAY.
I'M ALTO.
NICE TO MEET YOU. I'LL GO PICK UP SOME STUFF FOR DINNER AND GET IT COOKING. SEE YOU AROUND SUNDOWN, ALTO.

CHAPTER 3

OOF! SORRY—
UUGH!

HEY! WHY CAN'T YOU—
WATCH IT, EARTHWORM.

PARDON ME, GENTLEFOLK.
GAH!
MY TROUPE-MATES AND I WERE WONDERING IF WE COULD TROUBLE YOU FOR A MOMENT OF YOUR TIME.
I'M A *BARD*, YOU SEE, A FORMER APPRENTICE TO THE GREAT ELUVIAN HERSELF.
OH, ANOTHER BARD! I GUESS WE'RE IN LUCK TODAY.
HOW CAN WE HELP—
PERFECT, THANKS.
THIS WAY.

WHAT DO YOU NEED US TO DO?
NOTHING.
JUST STAND THERE AND LISTEN.

WHAT IS THIS?! WHAT'S—
HAPPENING...
FELL, THE SPELL IS *WORKING*!
OF *COURSE* IT'S WORKING. *I* INVENTED IT. NOW WATCH—
THIS IS THE GOOD PART.

ARRRGH!
LOOK AT THEM GO!
A SPELL TO SHAPE THE MINDS OF THE LISTENERS.
WE'LL USE THIS ON BRIGHTBLADE AND THE TROLLS, AND THEY'LL RIP EACH OTHER TO SHREDS.
WE'LL GET BACK *EVERYTHING* SHE STOLE FROM US.
SO IT'S READY? WE'RE HEADED TO THE PALACE?
NOT YET. THIS WON'T LAST LONG; THE SPELL ISN'T STRONG ENOUGH.
WE NEED TO SHOW THE WORLD THAT BRIGHTBLADE'S GRIP ON SKALD IS CRUMBLING. FOR THAT, WE NEED—

CRASH!
FELL, HE SAW US!
GOT YOU!

LET GO!
ACK!
HEHE...
UGH!
CRACK!

UUUUGH...
WELL, WHAT DO YOU KNOW?
THE LITTLE EARTHWORM KNOWS MAGIC.
M-MY--
LEAVE IT TO THE *REAL* BARDS NEXT TIME.

CHAPTER 4

ALTO?
COME ON, LITTLE GUY. WAKE UP!
...EBBE?
OH, AMAZING. YOU'RE STILL ALIVE.
I CAME TO FIND YOU AFTER YOU DIDN'T SHOW. I LOOKED ALL OVER THE PLACE.
WHAT...
I GOT WORRIED WHEN I DIDN'T SEE YOU AROUND WHEN THE MARKET CLOSED. WHAT HAPPENED?
IT WAS THOSE BARDS! AT THE MARKET!

THEY USED SOME KIND OF SPELL. I'VE NEVER SEEN ANYTHING LIKE IT—
OOOOGH...
TAKE IT EASY, LITTLE GUY.
YOU SHOULD COME BACK TO THE HEARTH WITH ME, AT LEAST UNTIL YOU'RE STEADIER ON YOUR FEET.

THERE SHE IS...
THE HEARTH. MY HOME, MY HEART, MY PRIDE AND JOY.

AND THAT'S KNUD. HE'S FINE, I GUESS.
MUNCH!
MUNCH!
WOW...
YOU *LIVE* IN THIS?
YEP. WANDERING THE ROAD IS EASIER IF YOUR HOUSE WANDERS WITH YOU, YOU KNOW?
YEAH...
HEY!
CAREFUL. KNUD WILL TAKE A TASTE OF ANYTHING THAT WANDERS TOO CLOSE TO THAT MAW OF HIS.

COME ON, I'LL GIVE YOU THE GRAND TOUR.
HOME SWEET HOME.
YOU HAVE SO MUCH NEAT STUFF IN HERE!
YEAH, JUST SOME THINGS I'VE PICKED UP OVER THE YEARS.
YOU'VE BEEN TRAVELING ALONE THE WHOLE TIME?

ME AND KNUD, YEAH. MY CLAN...WELL, LET'S JUST SAY THEY DON'T REALLY *GET* MAGIC.
SCRITCH
SCRITCH
SO HOW DID YOU LEARN IT?
WHEN I WAS A TINY GIRL TROLLKIN, MY CLAN WENT TO A LOT OF PEACE TALKS.
WE WERE TRYING TO FIGURE OUT HOW WE FIT IN, NOW THAT THINGS IN SKALD HAD CHANGED.
OLD ELUVIAN *HERSELF* WAS THERE. AT NIGHT, SHE'D PERFORM FOR US.
I'D NEVER SEEN ANYTHING LIKE IT. I WAS OBSESSED WITH MAGIC.
I STARTED MESSING AROUND WITH ANYTHING I COULD TURN INTO AN INSTRUMENT: BOWLS, TREE BRANCHES, REEDS, WHATEVER.

IT TOOK A WHILE, BUT I STARTED FIGURING IT OUT.
MY CLAN THOUGHT IT WAS A WASTE OF TIME.
YEAH, I KNOW WHAT *THAT'S* LIKE.
SO I LEFT. I SAVED UP MY COINS, MET KNUD, BOUGHT THE HEARTH. NOW I DO MAGIC WHENEVER I WANT.
IT'S NOTHING SPECIAL— NOWHERE NEAR AS FANCY AS WHAT YOU CAN DO.
BUT IT'S BETTER THAN NOTHING.
NOTHING IS EXACTLY WHAT I'VE GOT NOW.
DID THE BARDS YOU MENTIONED DO THAT?
THEIR LEADER'S NAME IS FELL. THEY WERE TRYING OUT SOME NEW MAGIC. IT CHANGED THESE PEOPLE.
IT *CONTROLLED* THEM.

I DIDN'T KNOW MAGIC COULD DO THAT.
ME NEITHER! THEY'RE PLANNING SOMETHING BAD FOR THE PALACE.
BRIGHTBLADE'S PALACE?! OLD ELUVIAN WILL MOP THE FLOOR WITH THEM.
BUT SHE ISN'T THERE! SHE LEFT ON A MISSION FOR MY MO— ER, LADY BRIGHTBLADE!
HOW DO YOU KNOW THAT?
I—I HEARD PEOPLE TALKING ABOUT IT. YOU KNOW, AT THE MARKET.
IF THESE BARDS REALLY DO HAVE NEW MAGIC, AND ELUVIAN IS GONE, THAT PALACE MIGHT NOT BE ABLE TO DEFEND ITSELF.
I'VE GOT TO DO SOMETHING.
I DON'T KNOW, LITTLE GUY. YOU'RE JUST ONE PERSON. THEY'RE A WHOLE TROUPE OF BARDS.
THAT'S IT!

YOU CAN JOIN MY TROUPE!
YOU HAVE A TROUPE?
I WILL IF YOU JOIN IT!
ALTO—
COME ON, EBBE! WE CAN BE A NEW KIND OF BARD. WE'LL BE HEROES! WE'LL WRITE OUR *OWN* LEGENDS!
ALL RIGHT. NO PROMISES, BUT LET'S TRY IT.
YES! THIS IS GOING TO BE *AWESOME*!

ALL RIGHT, *FIRST* WE NEED A NAME. I WAS THINKING "ALTO'S ADVENTURERS." THEN WE NEED TO FIND OUT WHERE THEY'RE GOING NEXT. FELL SAID THE MAGIC WASN'T STRONG ENOUGH YET. MAYBE—
WE SHOULD PROBABLY WORKSHOP THE NAME A BIT. AND WE WON'T BE ABLE TO DO MUCH WITH YOUR INSTRUMENT LIKE *THAT*, ANYWAY.
OH, RIGHT.
IF WE'RE GOING TO HAVE THE MAGICAL *UMPH* WE NEED, YOU'VE GOT TO GET THAT FIXED. I KNOW A GUY.
REALLY?! HE CAN FIX IT?
IF ANYONE CAN HELP YOU, HE CAN. HE'S A BIT OF A LEGEND HIMSELF.
PERFECT! LET'S GO NOW!
HIS SHOP IS IN THISTLEFALL. THAT'S A TWO-DAY RIDE AWAY.

WE CAN SET OFF FIRST THING IN THE MORNING.
COME ON, TROUPE-MATE. LET'S CLEAR A SPOT FOR YOU IN THE HEARTH.

CHAPTER 5
THISTLEFALL

WE'RE HERE, LITTLE GUY. RISE AND SHINE.
TAP!
TAP!

WHUMPH!
CR-CRACK!
WHUMPH!
CRASH!
WHAT?! WHAT TIME IS IT?
ALMOST NOON. I WAS ABOUT TO PULL OFF AND LET KNUD CHEW ON YOUR EARS FOR A BIT, SEE IF THAT WOULD WAKE YOU.

ALL RIGHT. I'M READY.
TING!
TING!

HELLO!
CAN I HELP YOU?

HELLO. I NEED MY MANDOLIN FIXED.
I'M CLARABEL. I'M AN APPRENTICE. MAYBE I CAN—
KLA-KLACK!
OH.
THIS IS PROBABLY SOMETHING MASTER CALDER WILL NEED TO LOOK AT.
AND HE CAN FIX IT? THIS MASTER CA—
WAIT, DID YOU SAY CALDER?
TING!
TING!
THAT'S MY NAME, BOY.

CALDER THE *CRUSHER*? FROM THE BRIGHTBLADE BALLADS?
DON'T WEAR IT OUT.
DID YOU FIND IT, MASTER CALDER?
I CAN'T FIND THE BLASTED THING *ANYWHERE*. IT TORE OPEN ANOTHER CHICKEN COOP. NOT A PRETTY SIGHT.
CLUNK
WHAT DID THAT?
SOME BEAST THAT'S BEEN CREEPING AROUND.
I CAME TO THIS TOWN TO GET SOME QUIET, TO MAKE SOME THINGS. BUT NOW THERE ARE MORE AND MORE BEASTS AND BANDITS POPPING UP THAT NEED DEALING WITH.

SO, WHAT DO YOU NEED?
UM, ALTO?... ALTO HERE GOT HIS INSTRUMENT A LITTLE KICKED AROUND. WE WERE HOPING YOU MIGHT BE ABLE TO FIX HER UP.
HMPH. THAT WAS CARELESS OF YOU. LET'S TAKE A LOOK.
HMM. PINK HAIR . . . YOUR NAME IS ALTO?
Y-YES?
WELL, YOU CERTAINLY DID A NUMBER ON THIS THING.
YOU CAN FIX IT, THOUGH, RIGHT?
NOT ANYTIME SOON. THE SHOP GOT BROKEN INTO LAST NIGHT AND THE THIEVES STOLE MY ORPHEUM ROSIN. I HAVEN'T HAD TIME TO GET MORE WITH THIS BEAST TEARING UP THE TOWN.
WHY WOULD BANDITS STEAL ROSIN? ISN'T IT JUST HARD TREE SAP?

THEY MUST KNOW A BIT OF MAGIC. ORPHEUM ROSIN IS GOOD FOR THAT.
YOU RUB IT ON AN INSTRUMENT'S STRINGS— THE TONE IT MAKES IS SO PURE THAT ANY MAGIC DONE WITH IT IS STRONGER.
KRICK
WHAT DID THE THIEVES LOOK LIKE?
IT WAS THE MIDDLE OF THE NIGHT. I DIDN'T GET A GOOD LOOK.
ONE OF THEM WAS WEARING A BIG, STUPID HAT.
I CHASED THEM AS FAR AS I COULD, BUT I'M NOT AS YOUNG AS I USED TO BE.
YOU HAVEN'T REACHED OUT TO LADY BRIGHTBLADE FOR HELP? I BET SHE'D—
SHE'S JUGGLING TOO MUCH ALREADY, AS ALWAYS. PEOPLE IN THIS TOWN NEED THE HELP NOW.

HOW IS YOUR MOTHER DOING, BY THE WAY?
MY MOM?
YOU KNOW ALTO'S MOTHER?
SHE'S—
A WOODCUTTER! SHE'S A WOODCUTTER. SHE MUST DELIVER TO THIS SHOP SOMETIMES.
RIGHT, MASTER CALDER? SHE'S DOING JUST GREAT.
...SURE. WHATEVER YOU SAY.
WHAT IF WE GOT THE ROSIN FOR YOU? THEN YOU'D HAVE TIME TO FIX MY MANDOLIN.
YOU'D HAVE TO GET THE SAP FOR IT STRAIGHT FROM THE TREE. THERE'S A GROVE OUTSIDE OF TOWN.

SO YOU'LL DO IT?!
AS A FAVOR TO YOUR "WOODCUTTER" MOM. BRING BACK ENOUGH AND I'LL THROW IN SOME EXTRA ROSIN FOR YOUR STRINGS.
HAMMER THAT INTO THE BARK. IT'LL MAKE THE SAP FLOW NICE AND SMOOTH.
GOT IT. WE'LL BE BACK BEFORE YOU KNOW IT!
AND DON'T GET EATEN BY THAT BEAST!

HERE. IT'S NOT MUCH, BUT AT LEAST YOU'LL HAVE SOME MAGIC IF WE RUN INTO ANY MONSTERS.
YOU CAN PLAY THIS, RIGHT?

YOU HEARD WHAT MASTER CALDER SAID? FELL WAS *HERE*!
HE SAID THE ROSIN MAKES MAGIC MORE POWERFUL. IF THEY USE IT WITH THEIR NEW SPELL—
BUT THIS MEANS THEY HAVEN'T REACHED THE PALACE YET!
THEIR SPELL STILL ISN'T FINISHED!
TAK!
TAK!
TAK!
TAK!
TAK!

WE'LL CATCH UP TO THEM, AND WITH ROSIN OF OUR OWN TO MAKE OUR MAGIC STRONGER . . .
. . . THEY WON'T STAND A CHANCE.
RRRRRR
THERE! NOW WE WAIT.
RRAAAARR!

ALTO!
SCEEE!

I THINK WE FOUND CALDER'S BEAST!
RRRRRRR
SCEEEE!
HISSSS
THAT'S GOOD, EBBE! KEEP IT BUSY WHILE I GET THE SAP.
WHAT? ALTO, *NO*!

COME ON, HURRY!
LOOK OUT!
RRRRRRRRRRRRRRRRRRRR
ACK!

HIIISSSS

CLARABEL?!
YOU CAN DO MAGIC?!
LATER! HELP!
I CAN'T SHAPE MY WILL WITH THIS. I NEED TO USE WORDS!
I'LL SHAPE IT. JUST PLAY!

SCEEE!

THAT WAS *EXHAUSTING.*
THAT WAS *AWESOME!*
HOW DO *YOU* KNOW MAGIC? HOW DID YOU SHAPE IT LIKE THAT? YOU DIDN'T USE ANY WORDS!
I USE THE MUSIC ITSELF TO SHAPE THE MAGIC. I'M NOT VERY GOOD AT LYRICS—I CAN'T SING.
BUT THAT'S *IMPOSSIBLE.*
I DON'T REALLY KNOW THE PROPER WAY. I'VE READ MASTER CALDER'S JOURNALS FROM WHEN HE WAS TRAVELING WITH LADY BRIGHTBLADE AND MASTER ELUVIAN.
HE SAW ELUVIAN BUILD HER TECHNIQUE. I'VE BEEN TEACHING MYSELF HOW TO DO IT FROM HIS DESCRIPTIONS.
LOOK AT US, A TRIO OF SELF-TAUGHT BARDS!

RIGHT. ALL THREE OF US.
YOU KNOW, CLARABEL, YOU SHOULD JOIN OUR TROUPE!
YEAH! I'M SURE WE COULD TALK OLD CALDER INTO LETTING YOU JOIN.
PLEASE DON'T TELL MASTER CALDER. HE DOESN'T KNOW I'VE BEEN READING HIS JOURNALS.
YOU THINK HE'D BE MAD? WITH MAGIC LIKE *THAT*?
I'M NOT MEANT TO BE *DOING* MAGIC. I *REALLY* NEED THIS APPRENTICESHIP.
PROMISE YOU WON'T SAY ANYTHING.
IF YOU WANT, BUT YOU SHOULD JOIN US ANYWAY. OUR TROUPE WOULD BE THE *BEST*.

CHAPTER 6
THISTLEFALL

VICTORY!
WE HAVE THE SAP!
TOOK YOU LONG ENOUGH. DID CLARABEL FIND YOU? I FIGURED YOU'D GET LOST.
WE WERE TAKING CARE OF YOUR BEAST PROBLEM.

WHAT? CLARABEL, IS THAT TRUE?
YEAH, THEY CHASED IT OFF WITH MAGIC. I DON'T THINK IT WILL BE BACK.
CLARABEL WAS VERY HELPFUL. IN FACT, WITHOUT HER SPECIAL SKILLS, WE MIGHT NOT HAVE MADE IT.
SHE'S CERTAINLY TALENTED. YOU'RE LUCKY YOU ALL WEREN'T EATEN. BUT YOU'VE DONE THE PEOPLE IN THIS TOWN A GOOD TURN, AND I WON'T FORGET. THANK YOU.
HM. THIS'LL DO. YOU TWO HAD BETTER FIND SOMEWHERE TO BUNK DOWN.
YOUR INSTRUMENT AND THE ROSIN WILL BE DONE IN THE MORNING.
I'LL BE HERE FIRST THING!

NO THANKS. I'VE BEEN WOKEN UP BY YOU BARD TYPES BEFORE. NO RESPECT FOR THE SANCTITY OF A MAN'S MORNING.
I'LL HAVE CLARABEL RUN IT TO YOU.
AND, BOY?
GIVE MY LOVE TO YOUR MOTHER WHEN YOU SEE HER.
UM . . . I WILL. THANK YOU.

THE NEW DESK LEGS ARE SANDED DOWN AND READY FOR THE CARTER COMMISSION, AND I PUT THE NEW BOWL SET OUT FOR THE VARNISH TO DRY. IS THERE ANYTHING ELSE, MASTER CALDER?
THANK YOU, CLARABEL. NO, THAT'S ABOUT IT.
THOSE BARDS ARE SOMETHING ELSE, HM? PEOPLE LIKE THEM ARE ALWAYS CHASING AFTER ADVENTURES.
YES, SIR.
BY THE WAY, I ORGANIZED MY JOURNALS TODAY. DON'T WORRY, I BOOKMARKED YOUR PLACE.
MASTER CALDER, I'M SO SORRY, I DIDN'T MEAN—
DON'T GIVE ME THAT, GIRL. AND DON'T THINK I DON'T KNOW ABOUT THE FIDDLE YOU HIDE OUT IN THE SHED.

A LONG TIME AGO, A GOOD FRIEND TAUGHT ME THE VALUE OF MAKING SOMETHING FROM YOUR HEART. THAT'S WHY I OPENED THIS SHOP.
THIS IS WHERE MY HEART IS, BUT I KNOW YOURS ISN'T.
SO, WHEN YOU TAKE THAT BOY HIS THINGS TOMORROW, YOU MIGHT THINK TO CHASE AN ADVENTURE OF YOUR OWN.
BUT MY PARENTS–
DON'T WORRY, I'LL TALK TO THEM. THEY'LL LEARN TO BE PROUD OF THEIR GIRL'S TALENT.
GET SOME SLEEP. YOU'VE GOT AN EARLY MORNING AHEAD.
...THANK YOU, MASTER CALDER.
GOOD NIGHT.

YOU'RE UP EARLY FOR ONCE.
I'M WAITING FOR CLARABEL. DO YOU THINK I SHOULD JUST GO TO THE SHOP?
SCRITCH SCRITCH

I THINK IF YOU WOKE CALDER AT THIS HOUR, HE'D BREAK YOUR INSTRUMENT AGAIN BY HITTING YOU OVER THE HEAD WITH IT.
WHEN IS SHE GOING TO GET HERE?!
CALM DOWN, LITTLE GUY. THE SUN IS BARELY UP. GIVE PEOPLE A CHANCE TO GET THEIR WHEELS TURNING.
ALTO!
EBBE!

IS IT DONE?!
IS THAT IT?!
YES, MASTER CALDER—
FINALLY!

WHOA.
DON'T WORRY. YOU GET USED TO HIM.
I ALSO WANTED TO ASK YOU— I WAS HOPING—
YES?
LOOK. I LOVE MAGIC. I NEED MAGIC. BUT MY FAMILY...
WE DON'T HAVE A LOT. THINGS HAVE BEEN ROUGH FOR A WHILE. MY PARENTS THINK MAGIC IS A WASTE OF TIME.
WHEN MASTER CALDER OFFERED ME AN APPRENTICESHIP, MY PARENTS WERE SO EXCITED TO HAVE ME LEARN A TRADE, TO BUILD A BETTER LIFE FOR MYSELF.
BUT I DON'T WANT TO BE A CARPENTER.

I WANT TO BE A BARD. I WANT TO JOIN YOUR TROUPE.
IF YOU'LL STILL HAVE ME, THAT IS. I MEAN—
WE ALREADY MADE ROOM IN THE HEARTH.
ALTO THOUGHT YOU'D SNEAK OUT IN THE MIDDLE OF THE NIGHT TO JOIN US. I FIGURED YOU WOULD NEED TO SLEEP ON IT.
HOW DID YOU KNOW?

ALTO HAS AN EFFECT ON PEOPLE.
I'M INCREDIBLY CHARMING.
WELL... THANK YOU.
WELCOME TO "ALTOTUDE"!
WE HAVEN'T SETTLED ON THE NAME.

CHAPTER 7

HOW LONG UNTIL WE'RE THERE?
THE SAME AS THE LAST TIME YOU ASKED. SOON.

AND YOU'RE SURE THIS IS THE RIGHT WAY?
MASTER CALDER SAID THE BANDITS HEADED SOUTH OUT OF TOWN. IF THEY'RE GOING TO THE PALACE, THE ONLY WAY IS TO LOOP THROUGH ASHVILLE.
IT'S A LONG WAY AROUND. DO YOU THINK FELL PLANS TO TRY THE SPELL AGAIN THERE WITH THE ROSIN THEY STOLE?
IF THEY ARE, IT'LL GIVE US THE CHANCE TO CATCH UP! WE CAN STOP THEM BEFORE THEY'RE ANYWHERE *NEAR* THE PALACE.
IF WE GET THERE *SOON*, THAT IS.
WE *WILL*.
IT'S BEEN A LONG TIME SINCE I'VE BEEN TO ASHVILLE. MAYBE ONCE WE'RE DONE BEING HEROES, WE CAN VISIT BRIGHTBLADE'S BATTLEFIELD. HAVE YOU EVER BEEN, LITTLE GUY?
NO. MY MOTHER NEVER COMES THIS WAY. WE WEREN'T ALLOWED.
YOUR MOM HAS BAD MEMORIES OF THE DARK YEARS, HUH?

I GUESS SO.
YOU KNOW, YOU NEVER REALLY TALK ABOUT WHERE YOU'RE FROM. WHAT WAS YOUR LIFE LIKE BEFORE ALL THIS?
UM, NOTHING SPECIAL. PRETTY BORING. JUST HELPING MY MOM OUT ON THE FARM.
DIDN'T YOU SAY YOUR MOM IS A WOODCUTTER?
IT—IT'S A WOOD FARM.
LIKE... A FOREST?
YEP. WE CALL THEM WOOD FARMS WHERE I'M FROM.
THAT'S A GREAT WOOD FARM RIGHT THERE. JUST PERFECT, YOU KNOW... FOR FARMING.
RIGHT... AND WHERE ARE YOU FROM AGAIN?

HEY, CLARABEL, *YOU'RE* BEING MYSTERIOUS. WHAT ARE *YOU* DOING?
WHAT? OH. I'M TRYING TO MAKE UP A NEW SPELL.
YOU CAN'T JUST *MAKE UP* A NEW SPELL. CAN YOU?
SHE PROBABLY CAN. SHE'S PRETTY TALENTED.
FROM WHAT YOU TOLD US ABOUT FELL'S CURSE, IT MAKES PEOPLE FEEL ANGRY OR SCARED.
I THINK IT'S POSSIBLE TO MAKE A SPELL THAT MAKES THEM FEEL BRAVE OR HOPEFUL.
HOW WOULD WE DO THAT?
I DON'T KNOW YET, BUT I'M CLOSE. IT WOULD PROBABLY TAKE ALL OF US TO CAST IT.
IF WE'RE GOING TO FACE FELL AND HIS GOONS, WE COULD USE IT TO UNDO THEIR CURSE.

WELL, AS THE *TROUPE LEADER*, I SAY WE BLIND THEM WITH MAGIC AND THEN EBBE HITS THEM *REALLY* HARD.
I TRY TO AVOID PHYSICAL VIOLENCE.

NYAAAA!

WHOA!

WHOA, KNUD! STOP!

THERE NOW, BUDDY. THERE. CALM, *CALM.*
SOMETHING SPOOKED HIM.

CHAPTER 8
ASHEN PEAK

WE'RE TOO LATE!
WE'RE JUST IN TIME! LET'S GET THEM.
ALTO, WAIT! WE NEED A PLAN!
GREAT. COME ON, HE'LL NEED TO BE RESCUED.

IT'S PERFECT! THE SPELL HAS MORE THAN ENOUGH POWER NOW. WE CAN KEEP THEM AT IT FOR AS LONG AS WE WANT.
WE'LL USE THIS ON BRIGHTBLADE, AND HER OWN PEOPLE WON'T TRUST HER AGAIN.
HEY!
FELL, LOOK OUT!

WH-WHOA!
HNNG!
HEY, IT'S THE EARTHWORM! CAREFUL, YOU ALMOST HAD ME THERE.
WHAT ARE YOU DOING ALL THE WAY—
YOU'VE GOT TO BE *KIDDING.*
YOU'RE *BRIGHTBLADE'S* KID?

WHAT ARE THE CHANCES? WE HAVEN'T BEEN PROPERLY INTRODUCED. I'M FELL, AND THIS IS MY TROUPE, "DISCORD."
YOU KNOW, EARTHWORM, YOUR MOM *RUINED* MY FAMILY. WE HAD A GOOD THING GOING WHEN THE PALE DRAKE WAS ON TOP. WE WERE *LOYAL*.
THEN BRIGHTBLADE GOT IN A LUCKY SHOT AND IT ALL WENT AWAY.
OLD ELUVIAN PEDDLED THE STORY THAT SHE WAS THIS BIG, BAD WARRIOR TO EVERY KINGDOM ON THE CONTINENT, JUST SO THEY WOULDN'T MESS WITH HER.
SO, I DID WHAT I HAD TO. I PLAYED NICE. EVEN ELUVIAN SAW I HAD A KNACK FOR MAGIC AND MADE ME AN APPRENTICE.
ALL I HAD TO DO WAS SMILE AND TAKE WHATEVER CRUMBS THEY OFFERED.

ALTO!
I'M DONE WITH CRUMBS.
I'M GOING TO MAKE THE WHOLE WORLD SEE JUST HOW WEAK YOUR MOMMY IS.
THEN *SHE'LL* GET TO SEE WHAT IT'S LIKE TO HAVE HER LIFE RIPPED OUT FROM UNDER HER. WHAT DO YOU HAVE TO SAY ABOUT *THAT*, EARTHWORM?

MY NAME IS ALTO. AND I'M GOING TO STOP YOU.
HMMM.
I DON'T THINK SO.
ALTO!

WE HAVE TO CLEAR A PATH!
I'M WITH YOU.

SO, UH, ARE YOU FOLKS ALL GOOD?
WELL. OKAY.

ALTO, ARE YOU ALL RIGHT?
I-I'M FINE. WHERE IS—
THEY'RE GONE!
COME ON! WE HAVE TO CATCH UP TO THEM.
WAIT! WHAT ABOUT ALL OF THESE PEOPLE?
THE SPELL WILL WEAR OFF SOONER OR LATER. DISCORD IS GOING TO BRIGHTBLADE'S PALACE! IF WE DON'T CATCH UP TO THEM NOW, WE'LL *LOSE THEM*. PEOPLE ARE GOING TO GET HURT!
PEOPLE ARE GETTING HURT *NOW*! I THINK THE NEW SPELL WILL HELP, BUT IT NEEDS *ALL OF US*.

I'M WILLING TO TRY IF YOU FOLKS ARE.
ALTO...
ALL RIGHT, FINE. WHAT DO I DO?
WE'LL NEED THE ROSIN FROM MASTER CALDER.
I HOPE THIS WORKS.

I'LL GUIDE THE MAGIC, BUT IT NEEDS FORCE OF FEELING AND WILL FROM ALL OF US.
READY?

COME ON, FOCUS!
I CAN'T FOCUS MY WILL WITHOUT WORDS!
SING ANYTHING!
WHATEVER MAKES YOU FEEL INSPIRED.

THE THREE FOUGHT SIDE BY SIDE BY SIDE—
THROUGH A LAND TURNED HARD AND BLEAK.
BRIGHTBLADE'S FIERCE HOPE SERVED AS THEIR GUIDE—
AS THEY CLIMBED THE PALE DRAKE'S PEAK.

WHAT...
WHAT IS THIS? IT'S...
BEAUTIFUL.

IT WORKED! IT ACTUALLY WORKED!
WE DID IT!
YEAH...

CHAPTER 9
ASHEN PEAK

THE
LAST STAND

I'VE NEVER SEEN ANYTHING LIKE IT. EVEN OLD ELUVIAN HAS NEVER DONE MAGIC LIKE *THAT*.
I FELT SO LIGHT ALL OF A SUDDEN, LIKE A WEIGHT HAD BEEN TAKEN OFF MY CHEST.
I WASN'T SURE IT WOULD WORK. WE'D NEVER REALLY TRIED IT BEFORE.
SO THE SPELL WAS YOUR INVENTION? THAT'S INCREDIBLE!
ACTUALLY, WE'RE A TROUPE, "THE ALTONES," SO IT'S KIND OF ALL OF OUR INVENTION.
IN FACT, I'M THE TROUPE LEADER, SO IF YOU REALLY THINK ABOUT IT–
WHAT IS YOUR NAME AGAIN?
UM, IT'S CLARABEL.

CHEERS TO CLARABEL!
TO CLARABEL AND HER CREW!
TO CLARABEL!
TO CLARABEL AND HER CREW!
WELL, ENJOY "YOUR CREW," CLARABEL. I'M MORE OF A SOLO BARD, ANYWAY.
ALTO?

ALTO? THAT WASN'T COOL OF YOU BACK THERE. YOU—
ALTO?!
YOU'RE A *PRINCE*?!
NO. I MEAN, YES, TECHNICALLY, BUT NOT ANYMORE! I'M A *BARD*. THIS IS WHY I DIDN'T TELL YOU. I *KNEW* YOU'D LOOK AT ME DIFFERENTLY.
LADY BRIGHTBLADE, *THE* LADY BRIGHTBLADE, IS YOUR MOTHER? AND SHE LET YOU TRAVEL ALONE?

NOT EXACTLY. I RAN AWAY.
OH. UH, ARE WE IN TROUBLE? ARE PEOPLE GOING TO THINK WE KIDNAPPED THE PRINCE?
I'M *NOT* A PRINCE! I JUST WANT TO BE A BARD!
NO, THAT'S NOT TRUE. I DIDN'T JUST WANT TO BE A BARD. I WANTED TO BE A *HERO*. I WANTED TO DO SOMETHING GREAT ON MY OWN.
I THOUGHT IF I COULD SAVE THE KINGDOM WITH *MY* MAGIC, I WOULD PROVE TO MY MOM THAT—THAT—
I DON'T KNOW WHAT. IT DOESN'T MATTER. DISCORD GOT AWAY. EVEN TRAINING WITH MASTER ELUVIAN, MY MAGIC STILL ISN'T ANYTHING LIKE WHAT YOU TWO CAN DO. I FAILED.

YOU'RE RIGHT. YOUR MAGIC ISN'T LIKE OURS. YOU SHOULD FINISH THE SONG.
WHAT?
THE SONG YOU WERE SINGING DURING THE FIGHT. I WANT YOU TO FINISH IT.
IT'S JUST THE BRIGHTBLADE BALLAD.
I KNOW. AND I CAN'T SING. SO YOU DO IT.
BRIGHTBLADE'S PATH STRETCHED OUT BEFORE HER, THE WAY WOUND LONG AND LONELY.
ALL SHE KNEW LAY WRECKED BEHIND HER, SHE HELD THOSE MEMORIES CLOSELY.

SHE STALKED THE DRAGON TO HIS DEN—
HER HEART SET ON THE SNAKE'S END.
SHE BATTLED PAST THE DRAGON'S MEN. AS SHE FOUGHT, SHE FOUND HER FRIENDS.
THE FIRST, A MAN OF STEELY MIGHT, CALDER'S HAMMER WOULD STRIKE TRUE.
SECOND, A GIRL, HER SONGS ALIGHT WITH DREAMS OF A WORLD MADE NEW.

THE THREE FOUGHT SIDE BY SIDE BY SIDE—
THROUGH A LAND TURNED HARD AND BLEAK.
BRIGHTBLADE'S FIERCE HOPE SERVED AS THEIR GUIDE AS THEY CLIMBED THE PALE DRAKE'S PEAK.

THE SPELL WORKED BECAUSE WE GAVE IT OUR INSPIRATION. THAT SONG *INSPIRES* YOU.
YEAH, BUT—
YOU WANT TO BE A HERO LIKE YOUR MOM. BUT YOUR MOM *WASN'T* A HERO, NOT ON HER OWN. SHE HAD MASTERS CALDER AND ELUVIAN.
THEY SUCCEEDED *TOGETHER*. AND SO WILL WE.
IT'S NOT TOO LATE— WE CAN STILL CATCH UP. WE CAN STILL WRITE OUR OWN LEGEND.
YEAH. OKAY.

I'M SORRY. I'VE BEEN ACTING LIKE A JERK. AND I SHOULD HAVE TOLD YOU ABOUT MY MOM.
IT'S OKAY. I CAN'T REALLY PICTURE YOU AS A PRINCE ANYWAY. I'VE HEARD HOW YOU SNORE.
SO, WE SHOULD *REALLY* NAME OUR TROUPE. WHAT DO YOU THINK, CLARABEL?
YOU WANT ME TO NAME IT?
"CLARABEL'S CREW"? "CLARABEL AND THE CANTRIPS"?
WELL, IF WE'RE HONEST, THE NEW SPELL WAS YOUR IDEA.
SEEMS FAIR.
WHAT ABOUT SOMETHING WITH THE HEARTH? WE'VE WANDERED AROUND IN IT SO MUCH TOGETHER, IT WOULD MAKE SENSE.
"THE WANDERING HEARTH." I LIKE THAT.

HM. IT DOESN'T HAVE AS MUCH KICK AS I WOULD HAVE DONE. BUT I THINK IT'S A GOOD NAME.
ALL RIGHT. "THE WANDERING HEARTH" IT IS.
WELL, TROUPE-MATES, SHOULD WE GO AND SAVE THE KINGDOM?

CHAPTER 10
DAWN'S BAY

IT DOESN'T *LOOK* LIKE THE PLACE IS TEARING ITSELF APART.
THEY MUST BE PLANNING TO STRIKE DURING THE FESTIVAL CONCERT. THE CROWD IS GOING TO BE ENORMOUS.
SO, WHAT'S THE PLAN? SEARCH THE AREA, CATCH THEM BEFORE IT STARTS?
IF WE'RE LUCKY.
IF NOT, I DON'T THINK I'D BE ABLE TO SHAPE OUR SPELL LARGE ENOUGH TO GET EVERYONE AT THE CONCERT.
HONESTLY, WE COULD USE SOME HELP.

SHE'S GOING TO BE *REALLY* MAD AT ME.
SHE'S *LADY BRIGHTBLADE*, ALTO. WE'RE THE ONES WITH MAGIC, SURE. BUT SHE'S, YOU KNOW, *HER*.
ALL RIGHT. I'LL GO FIND MY MOM. BUT DON'T BLAME *ME* IF SHE DECIDES TO LOCK US ALL IN A DUNGEON.
SHE WOULDN'T *REALLY* DO THAT. WOULD SHE?

WE DON'T KNOW WHERE DISCORD WILL BE OR EXACTLY WHAT THEY'RE PLANNING. BE CAREFUL.
I'M *ALWAYS* CAREFUL.
DO YOU THINK HE HEARS HIMSELF WHEN HE SAYS THINGS LIKE THAT?

MOTHER!
ASTRID? WHAT IS—
ALTO!

AH, THE ERRANT PRINCE RETURNS AT LAST! HE STILL HAS ALL OF HIS LIMBS AND EVERYTHING!
PLEASE EXCUSE ME, CHIEF DAGDA. I HAVE TO TALK WITH MY SON.
HI, MOM. LOOK, I'M SORRY—

THANK GOODNESS. ALTO, I'M SO GLAD YOU'RE SAFE.
AW, MOM, I'M FINE. I—
OW!
OW! OW! LET GO! I'M SORRY, OKAY? OW!

EXPLAIN YOURSELF. *NOW.*
I'M REALLY SORRY, OKAY?
I SHOULD HAVE SAID SOMETHING BEFORE I LEFT. BUT WE DON'T HAVE *TIME* RIGHT NOW! THERE ARE BARDS WHO—
NO. I WILL *NOT* BE DISTRACTED. DO YOU REALIZE HOW *WORRIED* I'VE BEEN?!
I'VE HAD PEOPLE SEARCHING THE AREA FOR MILES. CHIEF DAGDA HAS BEEN WAITING HERE THE *WHOLE TIME*. I'VE HAD TO DELAY NEGOTIATIONS SO I COULD LOOK FOR YOU.
DO YOU REALIZE HOW MUCH TROUBLE YOU'VE PUT EVERYONE TO?
MOTHER, PLEASE! WE DON'T HAVE TIME—
NO, YOU'RE RIGHT. WE DON'T.
TONIGHT IS A TIME FOR THE KINGDOM AND FOR THIS FAMILY TO CELEBRATE TOGETHER, AND NOW THAT YOU'RE SAFE, WE CAN.
PERHAPS THIS FESTIVAL WILL MARK A NEW FUTURE FOR ALL OF US.
BUT TOMORROW, WE *WILL* BE DISCUSSING YOUR PUNISHMENT, YOUNG MAN.

WHAT *HAPPENED* TO YOU?
EXCUSE ME?
YOU USED TO CARE ABOUT BEING OUT IN THE WORLD AND *HELPING* PEOPLE. THERE ARE PEOPLE ABOUT TO ATTACK THE KINGDOM *RIGHT NOW*, AND ALL YOU CARE ABOUT ARE YOUR DUMB NEGOTIATIONS!
THIS IS WHAT YOU'VE NEVER UNDERSTOOD, ALTO.
WE FOUGHT SO HARD, FOR SO LONG, SO THERE WOULDN'T *NEED* TO BE ANY MORE BATTLES. THESE NEGOTIATIONS ARE THE BEST WAY I HELP PEOPLE *NOW*.
BUT IT'S NOT ENOUGH! I'VE BEEN OUT THERE, MOM! I'VE SEEN HOW BAD IT STILL IS!
THERE ARE MONSTERS AND BANDITS. THERE ARE PEOPLE TEARING EACH OTHER'S LIVES APART, AND NO ONE IS DOING *ANYTHING* ABOUT IT!
WHAT WOULD YOU HAVE ME DO, ALTO? I CAN'T BE EVERYWHERE AT ONCE. AS MUCH AS I WOULD LOVE TO HOLD THE HAND OF EVERY PERSON IN SKALD, I *CAN'T*.

THEN LET ME HELP! I'M IN A TROUPE NOW, AND WE—
THE BEST WAY FOR YOU TO HELP ME IS TO STAY *HERE*. YOU HELP BY BEING *SAFE*.
BUT WE'RE *NOT* SAFE!
I NEED TO GO GREET THE FESTIVAL PERFORMERS, AND THIS FAMILY NEEDS TO SHOW A UNITED FRONT, ESPECIALLY IN FRONT OF THE TROLLS.
IF YOU'RE GOING TO BE DIFFICULT, YOU'LL HAVE TO WAIT IN YOUR ROOM UNTIL I CAN DEAL WITH YOU.
PLEASE ESCORT MY SON TO HIS ROOM.
YES, MA'AM.
NO, WAIT!
MOTHER, WAIT!

CHAPTER 11
DAWN'S
BAY

COME ON, SKALD IS IN DANGER! YOU'VE GOT TO LET ME GET BACK THERE. I'M LADY BRIGHTBLADE'S SON, THAT MEANS YOU *HAVE* TO DO WHAT I SAY!
NO OFFENSE, BUT I'M *WAY* MORE SCARED OF YOUR MOM THAN I AM OF YOU. *I* DON'T WANT TO BE THE ONE IN TROUBLE.
ALL RIGHT, FINE! I'M *GOING*. YOU DON'T HAVE TO MANHANDLE ME.
THAT'S BETTER. I'VE GOT A SON ABOUT YOUR AGE, AND HE DOESN'T RESPECT—

AARGH!
JUST LIKE MY SON!
IT'S MY GREAT PLEASURE TO OPEN THIS YEAR'S SUMMER'S END FESTIVAL.
IT'S AN AUSPICIOUS YEAR, AS WE HAVE THE HONOR OF HOSTING CHIEF DAGDA AND THE TROLL DELEGATION.

MAY THIS FESTIVAL MARK THE BEGINNING OF A BRIGHTER FUTURE FOR US ALL.
NOW, I'M DELIGHTED TO BEGIN THE FESTIVAL'S CELEBRATIONS...
...WITH A PERFORMANCE BY THE LEGENDARY SVEN FROGTHROAT!
CLAP! CLAP! CLAP! CLAP! CLAP! CLAP! CLAP!
CLAP!
CLAP!
HEEEEP—
HRRRK!

ACTUALLY, *WE'D* LIKE THE HONOR OF KICKING OFF THIS PARTY.
MOM!
LADY BRIGHTBLADE. I DON'T SUPPOSE YOU REMEMBER ME, DO YOU?
I'M SORRY. REMIND ME WHERE WE'VE MET?
I WAS JUST A KID THEN. I OWE YOU A LOT...
...AND I THINK IT'S TIME I PAID YOU BACK.

SO MUCH FOR THE LEGEND OF LADY BRIGHTBLADE!
MOTHER!

NO, NO—
NO!
HEY, THE EARTHWORM IS STILL ALIVE!
DO YOU STILL WANT TO STOP ME?
COME ON, NOW'S YOUR CHANCE. THIRD TIME'S THE CHARM, RIGHT?

HA! THAT'S RIGHT, EARTHWORM. RUN AWAY!
RUN!

CHAPTER 12
DAWN'S BAY

EBBE! CLARABEL!
COME ON, WHERE ARE YOU?!
PLEASE, I CAN'T—

CLARABEL! EBBE!
WAKE UP! *PLEASE* WAKE UP!
I DON'T KNOW WHAT TO DO. EVERYTHING HAS GONE WRONG.
PLEASE, I CAN'T DO THIS *ALONE*.

A-ALTO, YOU'RE HURTING MY NECK.
YOU'RE OKAY!
OOMPH! NOW YOU'RE HURTING MY LUNGS!
OUCH.
ALTO, IT WAS *DISCORD*! WE FOUND THEM CREEPING AROUND BACK HERE, AND—
I KNOW. WE'RE TOO LATE. MY MOM IS UNDER THEIR CURSE. I COULDN'T STOP THEM IN TIME.

OH NO.
OKAY. ALL RIGHT. LET'S CALM DOWN. DO WE STILL HAVE THE ORPHEUM ROSIN?
I'VE GOT IT.
DO YOU REALLY THINK THIS WILL WORK?
WE'LL BE FIGHTING AGAINST DISCORD'S SPELL *WHILE* THEY'RE CASTING IT.
I THINK WE'LL HAVE A BETTER CHANCE IF WE CAN STOP THEIR MAGIC FIRST. THEN WE CAN UNDO THE DAMAGE.

ALTO, ARE YOU OKAY?
I'VE NEVER SEEN MY MOM LIKE THAT. I THOUGHT SEEING HER IN ACTION WOULD BE EXCITING. BUT IT'S *SCARY*.
WE'RE HERE WITH YOU, LITTLE GUY.
WE'LL MAKE THINGS RIGHT.

THIS IS *EASY*. THESE PEOPLE WERE READY TO BOIL OVER EVEN *WITHOUT* MAGIC.
BRIGHTBLADE IS GOING TO RUIN HER OWN KINGDOM. SHE'LL NEVER—
RIIIP!
OOMPH!

ALL RIGHT,
NOW OR NEVER!
WE HAVE TO
GET AS MANY PEOPLE
AS WE CAN WITHIN
THE SPELL!

THE WIND WHIPPED CRUELLY FROM THE PEAK—
HARD AS IRON, COLD AS HEARTBREAK.
LADY BRIGHTBLADE, HER STRENGTH WORN THIN—
HAD SUFFERED ALL THAT SHE COULD TAKE.

STRUGGLING UP TO THE DRAGON'S NEST, HER CLOSE COMPANIONS AT HER SIDE.
THEY'D TRAVELED FAR AND THROUGH IT ALL, THEIR LOVE AND HOPE HAD BEEN THEIR GUIDE.

WHAT'S HAPPENING—
NO, *NO*! IT'S TOO *SOON*!
YOU'RE *KIDDING* ME!

GET UP, YOU IDIOTS! WE HAVE TO RECAST THE SPELL!
UGH!

ALTO, WE NEED YOU! WE CAN FINISH THIS TOGETHER!
THE PALE DRAKE SAW THE HEROES COME AND DIDN'T TWITCH A WING TO FLEE.

HE SETTLED IN, ALL TEETH AND DREAD, SMILING AS LADY BRIGHTBLADE ROSE.
AND ON THAT STEELY DARKENED DAY, OUR LADY FOUGHT TO END OUR WOES.

ALL SHALL COME TO JOURNEY'S END—
DEFEAT FEARSOME FOES—
EMBRACE LOYAL FRIENDS.

IF WE PREVAIL, RIGHT THE WRONGS, WE'LL WEAVE THE FRAYED ENDS—
INTO TALL TALES AND BRIGHT SONGS.

ALTO? WHAT'S GOING ON?
MOM! IT WORKED. YOU'RE ALL RIGHT! WE—
SMASH!
YOUR STUPID FAMILY TOOK *EVERYTHING* FROM ME!

NOW IT'S *MY* TURN TO TAKE FROM *YOU*!
AACK!

HMMPH.
I'VE HAD ABOUT ENOUGH OF THAT.
YOU! YOU OLD *GOAT!* I'LL—
OOF!

KNOW WHEN YOU'RE BEAT, BOY.
MASTER ELUVIAN!
MASTER CALDER?
GOOD TO SEE THE ADVENTURING IS GOING WELL, CLARABEL.
I SWUNG BY AND PICKED CALDER UP ON MY WAY BACK INTO TOWN. I FIGURED WE WERE LONG PAST DUE FOR A REUNION.
IT TURNS OUT THERE'S MORE THAN ONE. THAT *IS* YOU, RIGHT, LITTLE FELONIUS?
YOU—YOU *HAG*! YOU OLD *WITCH*!
HM. STILL NOT VERY IMAGINATIVE, I SEE.

SO, IT LOOKS LIKE YOU ALL HAD FUN WHILE I WAS AWAY.
THE INSIDE OF MY HEAD FEELS SCRAMBLED. WHAT WAS ALL THAT?

I THINK... MY SON JUST SAVED US.
OUR WHOLE TROUPE DID. WE'RE "THE WANDERING HEARTH."

NICE NAME.
AND *SHE'S* A PART OF THIS TROUPE? I'VE NEVER HEARD OF A TROLL BARD BEFORE.
HEH. I GUESS I'VE ALWAYS BEEN A REBEL.
WELL, TORIL, IF THE CHILDREN OF OUR PEOPLE CAN WORK TOGETHER TO SAVE THE KINGDOM, THEN WE'D BE POOR LEADERS IF WE COULDN'T DO THE SAME.
WE'LL KEEP AN EYE ON *THEM* WHILE YOU TIDY UP THINGS HERE.
CONSIDER IT A RENEWAL OF OUR NEGOTIATIONS.
TH-THANK YOU, DAGDA.

ALTO, I—
THAT WAS *AMAZING*!
THAT MAGIC— I COULD *FEEL* IT IN MY CHEST!
HOW DID YOU LEARN TO PLAY LIKE THAT?

EPILOGUE
DAWN'S BAY
RAMBLE
THISTLEFALL
THE TEETH
HEARTWOOD
ASHEN PEAK

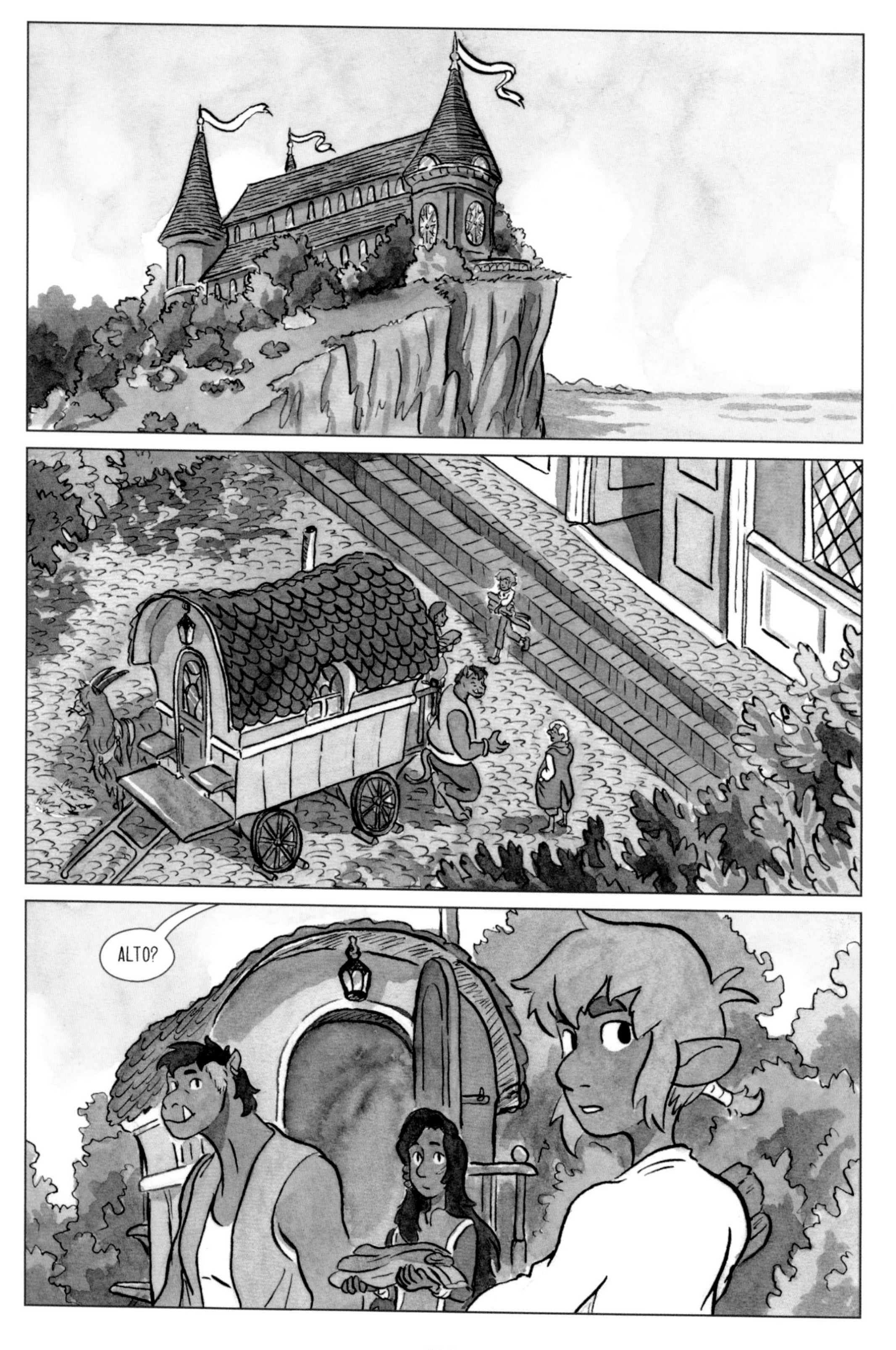
ALTO?

MAY I SPEAK WITH YOU FOR A MOMENT?
I HOPE YOU'VE PREPARED FOR YOUR JOURNEY. IT'S A LONG ROAD, AND TOWNS WILL BE FEW AND FAR BETWEEN.
YES, MOTHER. I THINK WE'VE GOT EVERYTHING.
AND REMEMBER TO PRESENT YOURSELF WITH DIGNITY WHEREVER YOU GO. EVERYONE KNOWS WHO YOU ARE AND WHAT YOU AND YOUR FRIENDS REPRESENT.
WHETHER YOU LIKE IT OR NOT, YOUR TROUPE WILL BE SEEN AS A REFLECTION OF THE KINGDOM OF SKALD. PLEASE KEEP THAT IN MIND.
YES, MOTHER.
WHA—I'M WORKING UP TO IT. DON'T RUSH ME.
nudge

LISTEN...
YOU AND I HAVE NEVER BEEN GOOD AT SEEING EYE TO EYE.
I HAVE TRIED TO BUILD THIS KINGDOM BY DOING AND SAYING THE RIGHT THING, AT THE RIGHT TIME, IN THE RIGHT PLACE. I'M *GOOD* AT IT. BUT WHEN IT COMES TO YOU AND YOUR SISTERS...
WHAT I'M TRYING TO SAY IS THAT I'M IMPRESSED WITH ALL YOU'VE DONE—
AND I CAN'T WAIT TO SEE WHAT YOU DO NEXT.
THANKS, MOM. I THINK YOU'RE PRETTY GREAT, TOO.
NOW, ON YOUR WAY. I WANT YOU SOMEWHERE SAFE BEFORE SUNDOWN.

FWIP
COME ON, TORIL, ADMIT IT. YOU COULDN'T *BE* MORE PROUD.
THIS ISN'T WHAT I EXPECTED. IT'S NOT WHAT I WANTED FOR HIM, EL.
YOU DIDN'T WANT HIM TO BE A *HERO*?
I DON'T WANT HIM TO *HAVE* TO BE ONE. WE FOUGHT SO *HARD*, FOR SO LONG. THE WORLD ISN'T SUPPOSED TO STILL *NEED* SAVING.
THE WORLD IS *ALWAYS* GOING TO NEED SAVING. IT WILL NEED DIFFERENT KINDS OF HEROES.

ALL WE NEED TO DO NOW IS TO GIVE THEM ROOM TO TELL THEIR OWN STORIES.
DO YOU THINK WE SHOULD GO OVER THE SPELL SOME MORE? WE STILL HAVEN'T TRIED IT IN AN ACTUAL PERFORMANCE.
WHY WOULD WE NEED PRACTICE? WE JUST SAVED THE WHOLE KINGDOM!
WE'RE PRACTICALLY MASTER BARDS NOW.
WELL, MASTER BARD, I'M SURE WE'LL FIND SOMETHING MORE CHALLENGING.

IT'S A LONG ROAD AHEAD, AFTER ALL.

ACKNOWLEDGMENTS

This book, like all books, was made with the help and support of many. First and always, thanks to my parents, Brad and Julia, and my siblings and their spouses, for nodding enthusiastically as I tried to explain the initial fragments of this story, and for always checking if my books are in stock whenever they're in a bookstore.

Thank you to Andrew Eliopulos for his faith in this story, and for doing so much to make it what it is. To Karen Chaplin, whose enthusiasm and expertise helped craft this story into something book-shaped. To Erin Fitzsimmons, Molly Fehr, Allison Weintraub, Shona McCarthy, Maria Whelan, and the rest of the team at Harper-Collins and Inkwell Management, for all of their hard work and skill. Their dedication to making beautiful books is an inspiration.

To Paul, Mikael, John, Alec, and Dexter, for telling interesting stories that never go the way I think they will.

The Legend of Brightblade was drawn and painted during the Covid-19 pandemic lockdowns, so a special thank-you to the doctors and nurses, the city, grocery, and delivery workers, and all other frontline workers who kept the world running as best they could.

The biggest thank-you to my husband, Matthew, for his wisdom, keen insight, and steadying support. His influence is threaded all throughout this book, for which I am incredibly grateful.